How can we make a musical instrument?

T0337059

Written by Susannah Reed

Illustrated by Janos Jantner

Collins

What's in this book?

Listen and say

tube

rubber bands

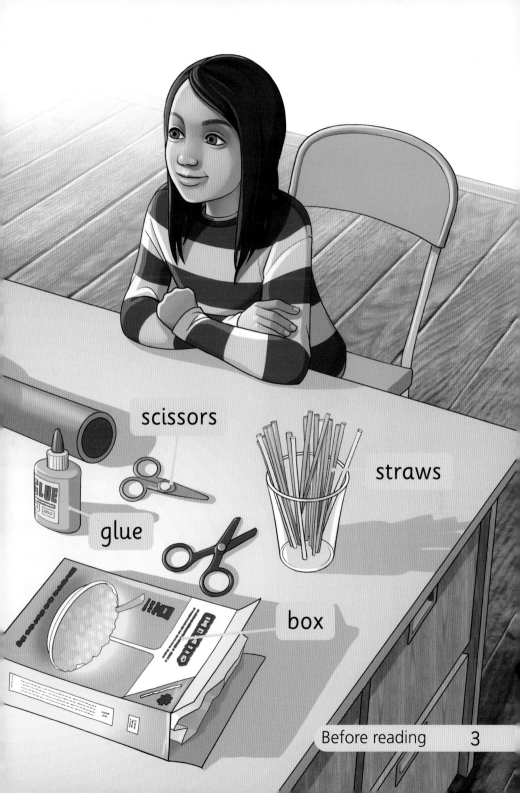

scissors

glue

straws

box

🎧 Zoe and Fred were in the town centre. Zoe said, "What fantastic music!"

musical instruments

Fred said, "I'd like to play music."
Zoe said, "Me, too, but we haven't got any musical instruments."

"We don't need to buy musical instruments," said their mum. "We can make some."

"How?" asked Fred. "How can we make a musical instrument?"

Let's make two musical instruments.
A shaker and a guitar.

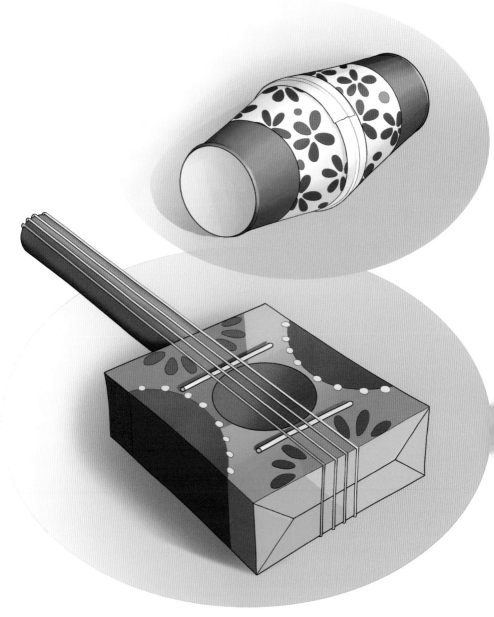

Let's make the shaker. You need two paper cups, some beans or rice, sticky tape, paints, paper and glue.

paper cup

beans

glue

rice

sticky tape

Paint the cups with different colours.
Or use glue to stick paper on them.

Put some beans or rice into one of
the cups.

Stick the two cups with sticky tape.

Now, you can play the shaker! Move the shaker up and down.

Make one shaker with beans and one
shaker with rice. Then shake them.
Do they make the same sound?

10

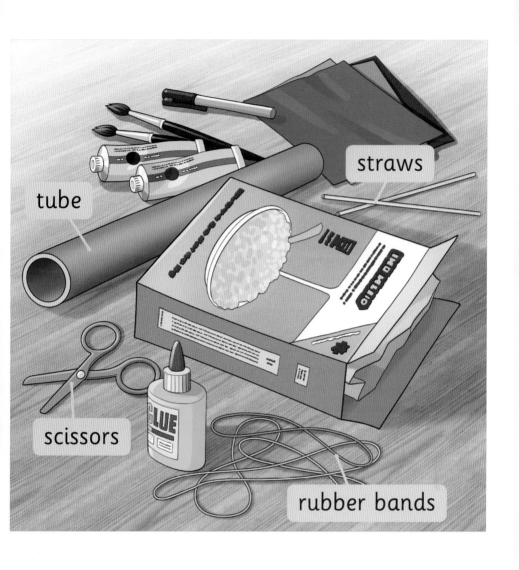

tube

straws

scissors

GLUE

rubber bands

Let's make the guitar. You need a box,
a tube, scissors, a pen, two straws, rubber
bands, paints, paper and glue.

Draw a big circle and a small circle on the box. Cut the circles. A teacher or parent can help you.

Then cut into the top of the tube.
Make eight small cuts.

Paint the box and the tube with lots of different colours.

You can stick paper on the box with glue.

Put the tube into the circle at the top of the box. Stick the tube and the box with sticky tape.

Get two straws and some glue. Cut the straws. Then stick them next to the big circle on the box.

Get four rubber bands. Put the rubber bands on the box and the tube. Put the rubber bands into the cuts you made.

Put one hand on the tube, and one hand on the rubber bands.

Now you can play the guitar!

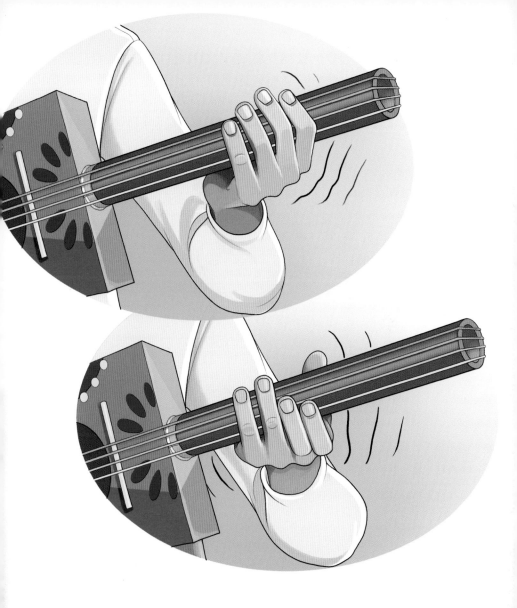

Move your left hand up and down the rubber bands. What different noises do the rubber bands make?

Now you've got a shaker and a guitar.
You can make music with a friend.
Which instrument do you want to play?

Mum asks, "What do you think?"

Fred says, "I want to make a
musical instrument!"

Zoe says, "Let's go home and make
one now."

Picture dictionary

Listen and repeat

box

guitar

paper

paper cup

shaker

tube

1 Look and match

sticky tape

glue

rice

rubber bands

scissors

2 Listen and say

Collins

Published by Collins
An imprint of HarperCollins*Publishers*
Westerhill Road
Bishopbriggs
Glasgow
G64 2QT

HarperCollins*Publishers*
1st Floor, Watermarque Building
Ringsend Road
Dublin 4
Ireland

William Collins' dream of knowledge for all began with the publication of his first book in 1819.

A self-educated mill worker, he not only enriched millions of lives, but also founded a flourishing publishing house. Today, staying true to this spirit, Collins books are packed with inspiration, innovation and practical expertise. They place you at the centre of a world of possibility and give you exactly what you need to explore it.

10 9 8 7 6 5 4 3 2

ISBN 978-0-00-839715-9

Collins® and COBUILD® are registered trademarks of HarperCollins*Publishers* Limited

www.collins.co.uk/elt

British Library Cataloguing in Publication Data

A catalogue record for this publication is available from the British Library.

Author: Susannah Reed
Illustrator: Janos Jantner (Beehive)
Series editor: Rebecca Adlard
Commissioning editor: Fiona Undrill and Zoë Clarke
Publishing manager: Lisa Todd
Product managers: Jennifer Hall and Caroline Green
In-house editor: Alma Puts Keren
Project manager: Emily Hooton
Editor: Barbara MacKay
Proofreaders: Natalie Murray and Michael Lamb
Cover designer: Kevin Robbins
Typesetter: 2Hoots Publishing Services Ltd
Audio produced by id audio, London
Reading guide author: Emma Wilkinson
Production controller: Rachel Weaver
Printed and bound by: GPS Group, Slovenia

MIX
Paper from
responsible sources
FSC™ C007454

This book is produced from independently certified FSC™ paper to ensure responsible forest management.

For more information visit: **www.harpercollins.co.uk/green**

Download the audio for this book and a reading guide for parents and teachers at www.collins.co.uk/839715